Star Friends

MIRROR MAGIC

To any of my readers who believe in
magic as much as I do…—L.C.

To Kim—L.F.

tiger tales

5 River Road, Suite 128, Wilton, CT 06897
Published in the United States 2020
Originally published in Great Britain 2017
by the Little Tiger Group
Text copyright © 2017 Linda Chapman
Illustrations copyright © 2017 Lucy Fleming
ISBN-13: 978-1-68010-458-5
ISBN-10: 1-68010-458-6
Printed in the USA
STP/1800/0435/0921
10 9

www.tigertalesbooks.com

Star Friends

Mirror Magic

BY LINDA CHAPMAN

ILLUSTRATED BY LUCY FLEMING

tiger tales

Contents

1

IN THE STAR WORLD

The sky was a velvet-black, and everything
glittered with stardust—the animals, the trees,
the meadows, the rivers, and the mountains.
They all shone. It was a special night, and a
large crowd of animals was gathered around
a waterfall made of stars that tumbled into a
bottomless pool. The air hummed with chatter
as they waited for the event to start.

At the front of the crowd there were eight
young animals—a fox, an otter, a badger, a
wildcat, a deer, a squirrel, a sparrowhawk, and a

mouse. The squirrel scampered over to the fox and stood up on his back legs, his shimmering tail curling like a comma behind him. "It's almost time for us to travel to the human world, Bracken."

"I can't wait!" the fox said, spinning around with excitement, his indigo eyes shining. "It's going to be such an adventure."

The deer's ears flickered anxiously. "Aren't you two nervous? I am."

The wildcat rolled her eyes. "What a surprise! You're scared of everything, Willow. Why don't you just stay home?"

Bracken gave her a look of dislike and touched the deer's nose with his. "Don't listen to her. You're brave, Willow, I know you are. And besides, we'll be together—at least to start with. You'll be all right."

Willow, the deer, nuzzled him gratefully.

A large owl with silvery wings swooped silently into the clearing. As he perched on a branch beside the waterfall, the crowd of animals fell silent. This was the moment they had been waiting for.

"Welcome, my friends," Hunter the owl called out. "Once again, the time has come for us to send a group of young Star Animals to the human world. Each of these animals will have the task of finding a Star Friend—a child who believes in magic."

Hunter looked at the animals around him and continued speaking. "These new Star Friends will be taught how to use the magic that flows between our world and the human world to do good deeds, bringing happiness and peace. As you know, usually only two or three Star Animals travel to the human world together, but today, eight will be making the journey." An excited murmur rose from the crowd. The owl held up his wing.

"We are sending more animals this time because the human world is in trouble. Fewer humans believe in magic, which means fewer people are using Star Magic to do good, and the current of magic that flows between our world and the human world is growing weak. But there's something even more worrying." The owl looked solemn. "We sense someone in the human world is using dark magic to hurt people and cause unhappiness. If this is so, it must not continue."

He turned to the young animals at the front of the crowd. "The eight of you will be sent to the place where we believe dark magic is being used—where the Star Magic is weakest. You must find out what is going on and stop it. But first, you each need to find a human child to be your Star Friend—a child who is kindhearted enough to use magic for good and brave enough to defeat someone using dark magic. When you meet a child you think could be a Star Friend, speak to him or her with your thoughts. If they are open to magic, they will hear you."

"What will happen to us when we're in the human world, Hunter?" asked the squirrel, jumping onto Bracken's back. "Will we still sparkle and shine like we do now?" He waved his tail, making every hair glitter.

The owl shook his head. "No, Juniper. You will look like a normal animal, except for your indigo eyes. However, unlike a normal animal, you will be able to appear and disappear."

"Will we all find Star Friends in the same place?" asked the otter.

"I do not think so," Hunter replied. "It is rare to find children who truly believe in magic these days, and there are unlikely to be eight such children in the same place. If you do not find a Star Friend when you arrive, then travel on. Choose wisely. Once you have found a Star Friend, you will stay with them for their whole lives, guiding and helping them and fighting dark magic."

The wildcat stood up. "When do we leave?"

"As soon as you wish, Sorrel," said the owl. "Simply step under the stream of stars in the waterfall."

"I'm going first!" said Bracken. "Good-bye, everyone!" He darted past Sorrel, who hissed at him in anger. With an excited bark, he leaped into the waterfall and vanished in a cloud of sparkles.

"Rude creature!" the wildcat spat. She gave a haughty flick of her tail, walked to the waterfall, and stepped carefully into the stars, vanishing. The animals' voices rose with excitement.

One by one the other young animals followed until, last of all, the mouse jumped through the waterfall and disappeared.

The owl turned to the crowd. "Let us hope our young friends succeed in finding Star Friends and defeating those who use magic for evil purposes," he said. "I fear that the human world needs Star Animals now more than ever."

He flapped his wings and soared away into the dark sky.

2
The Trouble with Violet

Mountain gorilla, orangutan, Galapagos penguin...

Mia Greene blew her dark blond bangs out of her eyes and turned the pages of the book on endangered animals. It was so hard to choose just one.

"Hurry up now, everyone," called Miss Harris. "There's just five minutes until recess. I want you to have decided on your project by then."

Mia turned the pages more quickly. Maybe

a penguin? They always made her giggle with their funny waddling walk. Or an African wild dog? She loved dogs. Or a wolf? She paused at a photograph of a gray wolf. Her Grandma Anne had loved wolves and had kept lots of wolf ornaments and paintings in her house. Mia's heart twisted in her chest. Grandma Anne had died last month, and Mia still missed her a lot. No, wolves would make her feel too sad.

"I can't believe you still haven't decided," said Violet, who sat next to her. "I've already done a whole page of notes on my animal." She flicked her strawberry blond ponytail over her shoulder and showed Mia a page of neat writing with headings underlined with a ruler.

"I have decided," said Mia defensively. "I'm going to do my project on … on … orangutans." She picked an animal at random just to get Violet to stop talking about it. Ever since they had been put at the same table at the start of the semester, Violet had been driving her crazy. It was bad enough that Sita and Lexi, her best friends, were in the other fifth-grade class, but having to sit next to Violet seemed very unfair. Violet was clever, and she loved pointing out any mistakes Mia made.

"Orangutans? Really?" Violet sighed. "Can't you be more imaginative than that? There are at least four other people doing orangutans."

"So what amazing, unusual animal have you decided to do your project on?" Mia asked.

"A pronghorn," Violet answered. "Do you even know what a pronghorn is?"

Mia hadn't ever heard of a pronghorn. Still, she didn't want to admit that to Violet, so she guessed. "Is it some kind of deer?"

She saw Violet's face fall slightly and knew she must have gotten it right.

"Kind of," Violet admitted. "It's a little like a deer and a little like a goat and a little like an antelope, although actually it's a totally unique animal. Anyway, why don't I find you something that's more interesting than orangutans?" She opened the book on her section of the desk. "Maybe you could do your project on a saola or a pangolin—they were my reserve choices—"

"Okay, everyone. Time for recess!" Miss Harris called.

Mia jumped up before she had to admit to Violet that she didn't know what either of those animals was. She put her books away and headed out of the classroom.

Lexi and Sita were waiting for her—Lexi, small and skinny, her curly black hair clipped back with a pink butterfly hair clip, and Sita, tall and graceful, with her shiny, dark brown hair in a thick braid.

"Escape at last!" Mia said, immediately feeling better at the sight of them.

"Your class was that bad?" asked Sita sympathetically.

"*Any* class sitting next to Violet is bad," said Mia.

Sita's eyes widened in warning. Glancing back, Mia saw that Violet had followed her to the classroom doorway with an open book about endangered animals in her hands.

"Well, that's the last time I bother trying to help *you* with a project, Mia Greene!" she snapped, and she marched back inside.

Mia felt a rush of guilt. She didn't like upsetting people—even people as irritating as Violet.

"Whoops," Lexi muttered.

"Wait here." Mia hurried back into the classroom. Violet was standing by their table. "Violet, I'm sorry…."

"Forget it," Violet said abruptly, picking up a book. "It's not as if I care what you and your silly friends think."

Mia bit her lip, not knowing what to say.

Violet turned her back. "I'm going to read," she said. "Go away."

Mia sighed and went back to her friends. "Well, that was awkward," she told them.

"It's her own fault," said Lexi loyally. "She shouldn't be so annoying. It must be horrible having to sit with her." She linked arms with

Mia. "Come on, let's go."

"So, what have you been doing this morning?" Sita asked Mia as they went toward the playground. The November sun was shining, but a cold breeze was making fallen leaves skitter across the ground.

"Miss Harris was telling us all about endangered animals," said Mia, zipping up her coat and burying her hands in her pockets. "She told us how many species are dying out and about how people need to do more to help…." An idea suddenly popped into her head. "You know it's the Harvest Show in the village hall next weekend? Well, why don't we ask if we can have a bake sale to raise money for endangered animals? We'll have all of vacation to prepare for it and do some baking."

"Let's do it!" said Sita.

"Great idea! We could bake a bunch of different cupcakes," said Lexi. "My dad is helping to organize the show. I'll ask him if he can reserve a table for us."

Mia beamed. "Perfect. If you come over tomorrow morning, we can choose which cupcakes we're going to bake and practice baking them."

"Okay, but it'll have to be before my gymnastics class at eleven thirty," said Lexi. "It's a cool idea, Mia."

Mia grinned. It really was.

Mia's mom was waiting for her in the car after school. She could see her 18-month-old brother, Alex, strapped into his car seat. He gave Mia a toy car as she opened the back door.

"Ook! Car!" he said proudly.

Mia grinned. "Yes, car," she said. She was glad to get out of the cold and into the warm car.

"Vacation starts now!" her mom said, smiling at her and starting the engine. "A whole week off. I bet that feels good."

"It does," Mia said. "No more Violet!"

Violet had spent half the afternoon ignoring Mia and the other half pointing out spelling mistakes in her write-up of a science experiment on onions that they had been doing. Mia's guilt over upsetting her that morning had soon faded.

Her mom frowned. "Oh, Mia, that's not very nice. You used to be good friends."

"In kindergarten and first grade, before she started being so annoying," Mia said.

It was true that she and Violet had gotten along when they started school. Violet was six months older than Mia, and she'd always had really good ideas for games—fun things, not just playing tag or hide-and-seek like everyone else, but pretending to be dolphins or imagining they had unicorns of their own. But then Violet had started to get really bossy, so Mia had made friends with Lexi and Sita instead.

"Can't you be friends again?" said her mom. "I was talking to Violet's mom, and she says

Violet is lonely."

Mia didn't believe it. "She doesn't act like she's lonely and wants to be friends with people. If we're all talking together, she just goes off and reads a book, and if she has to join in, she tells everyone their ideas are awful and hers are the best."

"It might be because she's an only child," Mom said. "I was one, so I know what it's like. It's sometimes difficult to know how to fit in. She might secretly want to make friends with all of you."

"Mmm," said Mia disbelievingly. She changed the subject. "Are we going right home?"

"No. We're going to Grandma Anne's house to collect some stuff for the thrift store. Dad's meeting us there, and then he'll go and pick up Cleo after basketball practice."

"Dactor!" shouted Alex, pointing at a tractor out the window.

"Yes, tractor! And look, there's a digger, too!"

said Mia, pointing things out as her mom drove
on through the twisty streets of Westport.

Mia had lived in Westport all her life—
it was a large city on the Pacific coast, and Mia
loved it. On sunny days, she and her mom, dad,
Alex, and older sister Cleo would go to the
beach and have picnics. On stormy days, they
would wrap up in raincoats and go for blustery
walks, stopping for a hot chocolate at the
Copper Kettle restaurant afterward.

Her mom drove across the main street on to
a small, bumpy road that led to the beach. There
were a few houses at the top of the road, and
halfway down was Grandma Anne's white stone
house with its pointed roof and small windows.

The car pulled up outside. Mia shivered. The
curtains had been pulled across the windows
ever since Grandma Anne had died. It made her
feel as if the house had shut its eyes.

Her mom got Alex out of his car seat and
carried him to the front door. Turning the key,

she pushed the door open. Mia followed her inside. The house was dark and cold, and there were moving boxes in the hallway.

For a moment, Mia pictured the house as it used to be—lights on, the smell of cookies baking, Grandma Anne standing in the kitchen making tea with her special red kettle that whistled when it boiled, the smile on her face when she saw Mia....

Mia backed out of the house. Being there made her feel too sad.

Her mom saw her face. "Are you okay?"

"Can I go for a walk?" asked Mia. "I'll just go to the waterfall."

"That's fine," her mom said, "but don't go any farther than that. Do you have your phone with you?"

Mia nodded and fled.

3
Something Magical

Mia hesitated at the side of the road. If she kept walking, she would eventually reach the beach. Instead, she crossed over it and headed on to an overgrown path that led into the woods opposite the house. Thorny bushes caught at her legs, their branches heavy with ripe blackberries. Mia edged around them and pushed through the drooping Queen Anne's lace. She breathed in the earthy smell and started to feel calmer. Pulling her coat closer around her, she hurried on down the path until

she emerged into a clearing. At one edge of it,
a waterfall flowed down a set of mossy stone
steps and then ran away in a gurgling stream.

Mia breathed out. The clearing was one
of her favorite places in the world. She and
Grandma Anne always used to come here. In the
spring, they had watched the birds and counted
the squirrels while the new leaves opened on
the branches. Now most of the leaves had fallen
from the trees, and the clearing was overgrown.

Mia wrapped her arms around herself and sat down on an old tree stump. It felt like everything was changing. *I don't like it*, she thought. *I don't want things to change.*

She swallowed as she remembered Grandma Anne sitting beside her, pointing out things. "That's a blackbird … and can you see the little wren over there? Oh, and look, there's a unicorn in the trees, Mia!" When Mia had swung around, Grandma Anne had laughed. "You missed it that time. But keep watching, and one day you'll see it, too—or if not a unicorn, you'll see something else magical, I promise. You just need to believe."

And Mia did believe. She would never admit it to anyone at school except for Sita and Lexi, but she did still believe in magic, even though she was in fifth grade. She squeezed her arms tighter around herself. *I do believe*, she thought to the Grandma Anne in her head. *I always will.*

"Hello," said a voice.
"Can you hear me?"

Mia's eyes flew open.
She looked this way
and that, but there was
no one around. She must
have imagined the voice.
But then her eyes caught
sight of movement in
the trees behind her. A
young fox with a rusty-
red coat came creeping
out. He had large
pointed ears, a bright,
intelligent gaze, a fluffy
snow-white chest,
and a bushy
tail that looked
like the end of it
had been dipped in
white paint.

Mia hardly dared to breathe. He was beautiful.

The tip of the fox's tail started to wag as he edged closer to her. As he got nearer, Mia saw that his eyes were a deep indigo blue. That was weird. She thought foxes had brown or hazel eyes.

Her phone rang, shattering the peace, and the fox raced away. Mia cried out in frustration and pulled out her phone. Her mom's name appeared on the screen. She quickly answered the call. "Hi, Mom," she said, her eyes searching for the fox in the shadows of the trees.

"Hi, sweetie," her mom said. "Dad's here, and we're ready to go now. Can you come back?"

"Um, yeah, sure," said Mia, still looking for the fox. He was gone. She sighed. "I'll come now."

She ended the call and, taking one last look, she left the clearing.

Her mom and dad were locking up the house when Mia got back.

"Hi, there," her dad called. "Ready to go home?"

Mia nodded, still thinking about the fox with the strange eyes. And what about the voice she had heard? She was sure someone had spoken to her in the clearing.

Her dad scooped up Alex into his arms. "Come on, young man. Into the car."

"Car!" said Alex in delight, hitting Dad on the head with the plastic car he was holding.

"Yes, car!" Dad said ruefully, rubbing his head.

"I thought I would stop in to see Aunt Carol on the way home while Dad and Alex pick up Cleo," Mom said to Mia. "Would you like to come with me?"

"Okay," said Mia. She liked Aunt Carol. The

elderly lady had been one of Grandma Anne's closest friends.

They got into the car and drove up the road to the main street. "Look, there's Violet," said Mom, spotting Violet in the front yard of her house. "Do you want to stop and say hi?"

Mia shook her head. "No, just keep going."

To her relief, her mom didn't insist.

Aunt Carol lived in a row of houses on the main street. She had gray hair and blue eyes that twinkled in her wrinkled face. When she opened the door to her house, the smell of baking wafted out.

"Well, this is a lovely surprise!" she said, smiling warmly as she saw Mia and her mom. "I wasn't expecting visitors today."

"We just thought we'd stop by and see how you were," said Mom.

"All the better for seeing both of you," said Aunt Carol. "Come on in. I've got some cookies here that need eating."

They followed her inside her cozy house. There were pictures of forest animals on the walls and a collection of crystals and polished stones on the dresser in the kitchen. Aunt Carol put the kettle on, and soon they were all eating freshly baked shortbread and talking about the memorial service that had been held for Grandma Anne two weeks before.

"The church was packed, wasn't it?" said Mom.

"Anne was very well loved," said Aunt Carol. "All her life. Right from when we were children. She was always the popular one."

"Well, she did love helping people," said Mom. "And she got involved in so many things here in Westport—raising money for charities, making the town more eco-friendly, saving the wildflower meadows."

"She's certainly going to be missed," Aunt Carol agreed. "Anyway, how are all of you? How's school, Mia?"

"Oh, okay." Mia caught sight of a little oil painting of a fox stalking some rabbits, and it made her think about the fox in the woods. "A really weird thing happened to me earlier," she said. She told them about the fox. "He came almost close enough for me to touch."

Her mom raised her eyebrows. "That's unusual. Foxes are shy creatures."

"Your grandma used to have a knack with wild animals," said Aunt Carol. "Maybe you take after her."

Mia liked that idea. "I hope I see him again," she said. "He had strange eyes—they were a really dark blue—like an indigo color."

"That can't be right, Mia," her mom said. "Foxes don't have indigo eyes. It must have been a trick of the light."

Aunt Carol gave Mia a thoughtful look. "Or maybe it was just a very unusual fox. I'd love to know if you see him again, Mia. He sounds fascinating."

Mia nodded, glad Aunt Carol believed her at least. "I'll tell you if I see him."

As the conversation moved on, Mia tuned out of the adult talk and thought about the fox. Sita and Lexi were coming over in the morning, but maybe she could go to the clearing again in the afternoon. She could take some pieces of ham in case he was there. She pictured him eating from her hands, looking up at her with those strange eyes. They *had* been indigo. She was sure it hadn't just been a trick of the light.

Maybe he's a magic fox. No. *That's silly*, she told herself. But her heart beat just a little faster at the thought.

4
MEETING BRACKEN

The next morning, Mia went to the kitchen and got out everything she thought they might need to prepare for their bake sale—recipe books, cupcake pans, and all the ingredients. The evening before, she'd told her mom and dad, and they thought it was a fantastic idea.

She had just finished getting ready when Cleo came into the kitchen in her robe. She looked around at all the baking equipment. "What are you doing?"

"Sita and Lexi are coming over for a practice

baking session."

"Oh, for the cake stand you were talking about yesterday. I'll make some brownies for you, if you like," Cleo offered.

"Thanks." Mia smiled. She and Cleo were very diffcrent—Cleo loved make-up, fashion, and gossiping about celebrities whereas Mia liked playing outside, baking, and making things with her friends. Still, most of the time, they got along just fine. Not like Lexi and her little sister, who argued constantly.

"What are you doing today?" Mia asked as Cleo made herself some toast.

"Seeing Beth. We're going shopping." Her phone buzzed and she checked it. "OMG!" she said. "Did you know Maddie and Jay have split up?"

"Who?" said Mia.

Cleo stared at her. "Seriously? Maddie and Jay? You know—the YouTubers?" Mia gave her a blank look. "How can you not know these things? Sometimes I can't believe we're sisters. I've got to call Beth!" She hurried out of the kitchen.

Mia shook her head. She just didn't get her sister's fascination with celebrities.

At nine o'clock on the dot, Lexi's mom dropped her friends off.

"I'll see you at eleven fifteen," she said to Lexi. "Make sure you're ready for me and changed into your gymnastics clothes."

"Yes, Mom," Lexi sighed. Her mom hurried back to the car, where Lexi's younger sister was waiting to be taken to her tennis lesson.

"You and your sister do so many things," said Mia as Lexi dumped her bag in the hall.

"Gymnastics, tennis, piano, swimming, math,

and French." Lexi checked them off on her fingers. "Oh, and now Mom wants us to start trampoline lessons, too."

"We'll never see you!" said Sita.

"Sleepovers," Lexi said decisively. "Even my mom can't schedule activities in the middle of the night."

"Sleepovers sound good to me," said Mia. "How about having one here the night before the bake sale?"

The others nodded enthusiastically.

"So, what are we going to bake?" Lexi said. "We need a plan!"

They sat down with the recipe books.

It didn't take Mia long to decide. "Chocolate fudge cupcakes for me!"

Lexi turned a few more pages. "I think I'll do lemon cupcakes."

"I'm not sure," said Sita.

Mia and Lexi started measuring out the ingredients they needed for the first batch of cupcakes while Sita kept looking.

"Watch out! Here comes the flour!" cried Mia, tipping the flour into the mixing bowl with a flourish. A cloud of flour flew up into the air.

"Mia!" exclaimed Lexi, pointing to the recipe book. "It says you're supposed to sift the flour into the mixing bowl, not just tip it in."

"Too late!" Mia grinned, wiping flour from her nose.

"But we should do what the recipe says," protested Lexi.

"I don't mind sifting it," said Sita reaching for the mixing bowl and carefully tipping the flour back into the bag. She was always the peacekeeper. "You two get going with something else."

"Okay. I'll prepare the cupcake trays," Mia said.

"So, have you decided what you want to bake, Sita?" Lexi asked as she started cutting butter into cubes.

"Not yet," Sita admitted. "I don't know whether I should do chocolate chip or carrot cupcakes."

"Chocolate chip," Mia decided for her.

"But…," began Sita.

"Nope, it's decided," said Mia firmly. She knew if she didn't choose for her, Sita would probably still be trying to make up her mind on the day of the bake sale!

They settled down happily to bake, and soon, three trays of cupcakes were ready to be put into the oven. While the cupcakes were baking, the girls started cleaning up, but when Sita flicked a dishcloth full of soap suds at Mia, it quickly turned into a water and soap fight.

Then they had to clean up the water and soap suds before Mia's mom came in. At last, everything was looking clean and neat, and the cupcakes were cooling on wire racks.

After Lexi was picked up by her mom, Sita and Mia began designing some posters to advertise their cake stand. When the cupcakes had cooled, they frosted the tops and decorated them with sprinkles.

"Mmm. Those cupcakes smell good," said Mia's mom, coming into the kitchen with Alex on her hip.

"Want one!" Alex exclaimed, wriggling and reaching out for the gooey cupcakes.

"Can he have one?" Sita asked Mia's mom.

"Well, I was about to make lunch, but a little taste won't hurt," said Mia's mom.

Mia and Sita cut up one of each type of cupcake for them to try.

"More!" said Alex, banging the tray of his highchair.

"I feel the same way," said Mom. "But we'd better wait until after lunch. You've done a great job, girls. I bet you'll sell a lot of these at the Harvest Show. Would you like to stay for lunch, Sita?"

"No, thank you. My mom is expecting me home," said Sita.

Mia and Sita packed two tins with cupcakes. Sita took one tin for her family and promised to drop off the other at Lexi's house. "I hope you see that fox again this afternoon," Sita said to Mia as she left. While they'd been making the posters, Mia had told her about her encounter with the fox and her plans to go back to the clearing that afternoon.

"I hope so, too," said Mia.

"Call me if you do," said Sita.

"I will," Mia promised with a smile.

After lunch, Mom drove to Grandma Anne's to collect some more boxes. "I'm going to the clearing, Mom," Mia said as she got out of the car.

"Okay. Don't be more than fifteen minutes, though—I'm just planning on grabbing some things and going. You have your phone, right?" her mom said.

Mia nodded and then hurried across the road and on to the overgrown path that led into the woods. *Oh, please be here!* she thought as she jumped over brambles and pushed aside the Queen Anne's lace. As she reached the clearing, a squirrel scampered down a tree trunk, and a flock of sparrows chattered in the branches. She looked all around, but there was no sign of the strange fox with the blue eyes. Disappointment washed over her. For some reason, she had felt sure he was going to be there. She sat down on a tree stump. Maybe if she waited for a while, he'd come back….

She blinked. The fox was there—at the edge of the clearing. It was as though he had appeared out of thin air.

Mia started to reach for the plastic bag with the ham, but he was already bounding over. He stopped and stared up at her. As Mia gazed into his dark blue eyes, she heard a voice say, "You came back."

Mia felt a rush of shock. The fox had just spoken to her, she was sure of it. But he couldn't have! Animals couldn't talk. She must be going crazy….

The fox continued to stare intently at her. "You can hear me, can't you? Please say you can."

Mia swallowed. The fox's mouth wasn't moving, but she could hear him in her head. It seemed impossible, but she knew she could.

"You can … you can talk?" she whispered.

The fox gave an excited yip. "You *can* hear me!" he said. "As soon as I saw you yesterday, I was sure there was something special about you. I felt it with every hair of my body. You must believe in magic."

"I-I do," Mia stammered.

The fox put his paws on her knees and licked her nose. "I'm Bracken. What's your name?"

"Mia," she just about managed to say. It was like she was in some kind of strange dream.

Bracken bounded away and then crouched

down in a play bow, his bushy tail waving in the air. "Hunter said we'd know! I can feel you're the right person for me. Will you be my Star Friend, Mia?"

Mia didn't have a clue what he was talking about, but this was amazing—awesome! Magic *was* real, just like Grandma Anne had always said. "Yes! I'll be your Star Friend," she said. "But … what is a Star Friend?"

Bracken trotted over. "There's so much I have to tell you. I come from a place called the Star World. Magic flows between our worlds, and I've come here to find a Star Friend, someone I can teach how to use magic. Star Animals help their Star Friends to do good deeds, and they stay friends forever."

Mia's thoughts spun. "So if I'm your Star Friend, you'll be with me forever, and I'll learn how to do magic?"

Bracken nodded, his eyes shining. "If you want to."

"Oh, yes!" What would Sita and Lexi say when she told them? A thought struck her. "Bracken!" she exclaimed. "My best friends believe in magic. Could they be Star Friends, too?"

"Maybe," Bracken said, looking excited. "The other Star Animals haven't found Star Friends yet. But to be a Star Friend, you have to really believe in magic. Don't tell anyone about it until we know whether they can be Star Friends, too. The Star World has to stay completely secret. We think there might be other people—bad people—who are using magic to do evil. The less they know about us, the better."

Mia's mind raced. "Okay. I won't tell anyone, I promise."

"Thank you!" Bracken bounded around her in a circle. "I'm so happy I found you, Mia. We're going to have so much fun together!"

He took a flying leap into her arms and licked her nose.

Her heart swelled happily. This was incredible! "I'll ask if Sita and Lexi can come over first thing in the morning. If they can, I'll bring them here."

Bracken nuzzled her. "I'll make sure the other Star Animals are here then, too."

"I'd better go now," said Mia. The last thing she wanted to do was leave him, but she didn't want her mom coming to look for her. "'Bye, Bracken. I'll see you tomorrow morning." Mia kissed him one last time on the nose, and then put him down and ran back to the house, her thoughts tumbling over and over in her head. She couldn't believe what had just happened to her. It was magic—*real* magic! This had to be the best day of her life!

5

THE SURPRISE

"Mom! Mom!" Mia gasped, bursting into Grandma Anne's house. Her mom was kneeling in the hall, putting some old diaries into a box. Mia skidded to a halt. "Please can Sita and Lexi come over tomorrow? I have to see them!"

Her mom smiled. "You can't be missing them that much. You just saw them this morning."

"I know, but this is important. I've … um … I've had an idea for a really good game in the clearing, and I want to play it with them. We could ride our bikes down here. You don't need to give us a ride."

"Okay. That's fine by me, as long as their moms are okay with it, too." Mom dusted her hands on her pants. "Aunt Carol is here. She popped in to see if I needed a hand, so we decided to do some more cleaning."

"Hello, Mia," said Aunt Carol, appearing in the dining-room doorway. She looked at Mom. "The china in the dining room is all packed up. I'll just check the cabinet drawers to make sure they're empty. Do you want to help me, Mia?"

"Okay," Mia said, following her back into the dining room. She felt like she was going to explode. If only she could tell someone what had just happened to her!

"I was thinking about you this morning, wondering if you'd see that unusual fox again—the one you were telling me about," said Aunt Carol, opening the top drawer of the cabinet and checking inside.

"I saw him just now," Mia burst out. She paced around the room, too excited to do something as boring as checking drawers.

"Really? And were his eyes blue?" Aunt Carol asked curiously.

Mia hesitated, remembering her promise to Bracken. Maybe she shouldn't say anything more. "I didn't get close enough to see," she lied.

"Maybe they are … and maybe he's a magic fox." Aunt Carol winked at her over her shoulder.

Mia stared. What did that wink mean? Could Aunt Carol possibly know about Star Animals?

Just then, Mia's mom came in with two cups of tea and a glass of juice on a tray. "Time for a break, I think. Thanks for helping, Carol."

"It's my pleasure, dear," said Aunt Carol,

checking the final drawer in the cabinet.
"All these drawers are empty now. Oh, wait
a minute. What's this?" She pulled something
out from the very back of the drawer. It was a

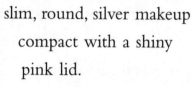

slim, round, silver makeup
compact with a shiny
pink lid.

"That's pretty," said
Mom, taking it and
opening it up. There was
a mirror on one side and a
pressed circle of makeup powder on the other.

"It is, isn't it?" said Aunt Carol, taking a sip
of her tea.

"Would you like it?" Mom offered the
compact to her. "It hasn't been used."

"Oh, no, I have no use for makeup on my
old face," Aunt Carol said with a chuckle.
"Why doesn't Mia take it?"

"Okay." Mia put down her glass and took
the compact. She had no use for the face

powder, either, but the case was pretty, and she liked the fact that it had belonged to Grandma Anne. She slipped it into her pocket. "Can I call Sita and Lexi now and see if they can come over tomorrow?"

"Sure," her mom said.

Mia went out to the front of the house, where the phone signal was better. Lexi was at her swimming lesson, so she left a message. Sita answered, though.

"So you want us to bring our bikes?" Sita said when Mia explained what she wanted.

"Yes. We're going to ride to the woods near Grandma Anne's," said Mia.

"Where you saw that fox? Did you see him again today?" Sita asked.

"You'll find out tomorrow," Mia said, hoping she was right. She ended the call and hugged the phone to her chest.

Oh, please let Lexi and Sita be Star Friends, too! she thought.

Mia was still buzzing with excitement when she got home. She danced around the kitchen, where Cleo was sitting at the table reading a magazine.

"What's up with you?" she said in surprise.

"Nothing. I'm just happy," said Mia.

She remembered the compact in her pocket and pulled it out, turning it over to look at it.

"That's pretty. Where did you get it?" Cleo asked.

Mia passed the mirror compact to Cleo so she could take a look. "It was in one of the drawers at Grandma Anne's house. Aunt Carol found it."

Cleo opened it and looked at the mirror.

"You can have it if you want," said Mia with a rush of generosity. "I don't need it."

"Thanks!" Cleo smiled. Her phone buzzed. She checked the screen and gasped. "No way!

Guess what's just happened to Beth!"

"What?" said Mia.

"She's been asked to model for a magazine! Oh, wow, I am *soooo* jealous!" Despite her words, Cleo didn't sound it, she just sounded delighted for her friend. She hurried out of the kitchen. "Beth!" Mia heard her squeal as she headed up the stairs. "That's awesome. What happened?"

Mia shook her head. If Cleo thought *that* was awesome, what would she think about what had happened to *her* that day?

She wondered if there were other Star Friends nearby and what their Star Animals were. Suddenly she remembered what Aunt Carol had said about Bracken being a magic fox, and a thought struck her. Maybe *Aunt Carol* was a Star Friend! And what about Grandma Anne? Could she have been a Star Friend, too? She couldn't wait to see Bracken again—there were so many questions to ask!

"This path is really overgrown," said Sita the next morning as she edged around a giant fern on the way to the clearing. The sky above was blue with wispy white clouds trailing across it. They'd ridden to Grandma Anne's house together and left their bikes in the yard.

Lexi jumped over a mossy rock. "Why is it so important that we come here today, Mia? What do you have planned?"

"It's a surprise," Mia said. Butterflies fluttered in her tummy. What was going to happen when they all reached the clearing? She remembered Bracken's words from the day before. *To be a Star Friend, you have to really believe in magic.* Lexi and Sita always said they believed in magic, but did they mean it? What if they couldn't hear the Star Animals speak? Then an even worse thought hit her—what if only *one* of them could?

Lexi looked at her warily. "You know I don't

like surprises."

"This will be a good one," Mia said, crossing her fingers.

When they reached the end of the path, Lexi and Sita looked around the clearing.

"Um…," said Lexi, looking confused. "What's the surprise?"

Mia chewed her lip. "Well…." She wasn't quite sure what she'd imagined would happen when they got there— maybe that Bracken and the other Star Animals would all be waiting. *I should have come up with a plan*, she realized.

Lexi and Sita were both looking at her expectantly.

"The um … the surprise will be here any minute now." Mia glanced around. "*Bracken! Bracken!*" she called in her head. "*I'm here! Where are—*"

Sita made a sharp intake of breath. "Look! It's a deer! Oh, isn't she beautiful!" A young deer with a coat gleaming like a chestnut stepped out of the trees. She stopped and stared at them with huge eyes, her delicate ears twitching. A red squirrel scampered down a tree and ran up beside the deer. It sat down on its haunches and looked curiously between the girls, and then an otter poked its head out of the river.

"There are so many animals here!" said Lexi as a sparrowhawk flew down from the trees and landed on a rock, a badger shuffled from underneath a bush, and a mouse ran out. Finally, a sleek wildcat with slanted eyes slid out from the shadows. All of the animals stared at the three girls.

"Oh … my…. *Wow!*" breathed Lexi, staring
around. "What's happening?"

"Is this the surprise, Mia?" whispered Sita.

Mia nodded.

"But how did you know these animals
would be here?" Lexi said in amazement.

Bracken came trotting out of the trees. Mia felt a rush of happiness as her eyes met his. He touched her hand with his nose. She heard him say, "Hello, Mia. Are these your friends?"

Lexi and Sita both gave strangled squeaks.

"That fox! He just *spoke*!" said Lexi, pointing at Bracken.

Mia looked from her to Sita. "Did you hear him too, Sita?" she asked.

Sita nodded wordlessly.

Delight rushed through Mia. "If they can hear you, that means they can be Star Friends, too, doesn't it, Bracken?"

Bracken spun around in delight. "Yes!" He turned and looked at all the watching animals—the otter, the squirrel, the deer, the hawk, the badger, the mouse, and the wildcat. "The question is—whose Star Friends are they going to be?"

6
CHOOSING A STAR ANIMAL

"What ... what's going on, Mia?" Lexi said
uncertainly.

"It's magic," Mia said in a rush as she looked
around the clearing at the beautiful animals,
all with sparkling indigo eyes. "These animals
come from another world—the Star World.
They're each looking for someone to be their
Star Friend. They'll teach that person how to
do magic to make good things happen." She
turned to Bracken in excitement. "That's right,
isn't it?"

He nodded. "Mia's my Star Friend," he told Lexi and Sita. "She said she thought you might both be Star Friends, too—and she was right!"

"I'd love to be a Star Friend!" Sita gasped, her eyes as wide as saucers.

"Where is this Star World? Can we go to it?" asked Lexi eagerly.

"No, I'm afraid not," said Bracken. "Only Star Animals can travel between the worlds."

"But you're saying we can learn to do magic here?" said Sita.

Bracken nodded.

"What kind of magic?" Lexi asked.

"That will depend on your own natural abilities," said Bracken. "But first you need to find out which of us is your Star Animal."

"Do we choose or do they?" said Lexi, looking around at all the animals.

"It can be either way," said Bracken. "But you both have to feel it in your hearts."

To Mia's surprise, Sita suddenly started walking toward the deer. "Hello," she whispered, holding out her hand. "I don't know how I know this, but I think I'm meant to be your Star Friend."

The deer sniffed her hand. She wasn't tall— her head was only just higher than Sita's hip and her eyes were huge, fringed with curling lashes.

"I think you're right," she said. "I feel like I know you already. My name is Willow."

"I'm Sita." Sita put her hand on Willow's neck, and Willow sighed happily.

Mia glanced at Lexi. Lexi was looking at the rest of the animals—the badger, the mouse, the wildcat, the sparrowhawk, the otter, and the squirrel. "You're all so beautiful," she whispered.

The squirrel scampered across the clearing toward her. "But I'm the one you should choose! I just know I am!" He stood up on his hind legs and stared at her with his small bright eyes. "I'm Juniper. What's your name?"

"Lexi," Lexi said.

Juniper leaped onto the tree trunk beside her, then onto a branch and hung upside down.

Lexi giggled. "I can do that, too." She did a handstand and looked back at him.

Juniper made a chattering sound as if he was laughing. "You're supposed to be my Star Friend!"

As Lexi turned the right way, Juniper leaped from the branch and landed on her shoulder.

A smile spread across Lexi's face as she

touched his soft red fur. "Yes, you're right," she declared.

Bracken yipped.

"The rest of us must keep looking for our Star Friends," said the badger rather sadly. "Come. We should move on."

The animals headed into the trees. The otter paused and looked back at the wildcat, who was still standing there. "Sorrel, are you coming?"

The cat yawned, showing sharp white teeth. "Maybe I will, maybe I won't. I'll decide for myself."

Bracken made a grumbling noise in his throat. "As always."

Mia glanced at him and saw he was looking at the cat with dislike.

The cat—Sorrel—stood up, shook her paws daintily, and then stalked into the trees in the opposite direction of the other animals.

"She seems kind of prickly," Mia whispered to Bracken.

The fox nodded. "She is. I'm glad neither of your friends chose her to be their Star Animal."

Mia turned to look at Lexi and Sita. Sita was petting Willow, and they were speaking softly to each other. Lexi was sitting cross-legged, giggling as Juniper ran up one arm, behind her head, and down the other.

Mia felt a burst of happiness. They were all Star Friends! "Can we start learning to do magic now?" she asked.

Bracken leaped into her arms. "You can, but first I think we need to tell your friends more about where we've come from."

Mia, Sita, and Lexi sat close together while Bracken, Juniper, and Willow explained about the Star World. Juniper sat in Lexi's lap,

Willow lay beside Sita, her slender legs folded underneath her, and Mia sat with her arm around Bracken, petting his thick fur.

"So, what's the Star World like?" asked Lexi.

"Beautiful," said Juniper. "Everything shines and sparkles."

"It must have been really hard to leave," said Sita.

"It was," said Willow. "But we wanted to come here to help. Humans need people in their communities who know how to use magic to do good, people who can solve problems, stop arguments, take care of the environment, and heal things and people."

"And we were told we were particularly needed here, in this area," said Bracken.

"Why?" said Lexi.

"The older animals in the Star World think someone might be using dark magic nearby," said Bracken.

"Dark magic," echoed Sita. "What's that?"

Willow's ears flickered anxiously. "Dark magic is the opposite of Star Magic. It comes from the ground, and it is magic that can be used to hurt people and make them unhappy. If someone is using dark magic near here, they must be stopped."

"Will stopping them be dangerous?" Lexi breathed.

Juniper nodded. "Yes. But we'll have each other." He rubbed her hair with his little paws.

Mia felt a mixture of excitement and nerves bubbling up inside her. Stopping someone from doing dark magic sounded scary but thrilling, too. "When can we start learning to do magic ourselves?"

Bracken jumped up. "Right now!"

"The sooner the better!" said Juniper, scampering after Bracken.

"Oh, yes!" said Willow, her dark eyes shining as she stood up. "We need to find out what your magic abilities are. Everyone is different."

"What do we have to do first?" Mia asked eagerly.

"Star Magic is all around you. It flows in a current, like a stream, from the Star World to the human world. You just need to open yourself up to it," said Bracken.

"How?" asked Lexi.

"Have any of you ever had times when you've felt completely lost in the moment?" Willow said.

"I have," said Sita. "Sometimes when I lie on the heather up on the clifftops with the sun on my face, everything else in the world just seems to fade away."

"That's happened to me, too," said Mia, remembering times when she'd been lying on the beach or sitting in the clearing, watching the waterfall.

"And me—when I've been floating in the water," said Lexi. "Or sometimes when I'm playing a piece of music I really love, I feel like I get lost in it."

Juniper waved his tail. "That's exactly the feeling you need to find now—exist in the moment, open your hearts, and the Star Magic will flood in."

"Don't try and *make* it happen, just *let* it happen," advised Willow. "If you think about it too much, I don't think it'll work."

Mia looked around at the others. "Come on! Let's try!"

7
LEARNING MAGIC

Mia, Lexi, and Sita shut their eyes.

Forget everything, Mia told herself. She tried
to push all her thoughts out of her head, but
for some reason, she found herself picturing
what she might have for lunch—sandwiches,
maybe, or pizza.... She shook her head. No. She
needed to concentrate. If she didn't, the others
would start doing magic and she wouldn't be
able to. That would be awful. She pictured Sita
and Lexi doing amazing things while she just
watched....

"Mia." She heard Bracken's voice. "Don't think about anything else. Just focus on being here, in this moment."

Mia took a deep breath and focused on the clearing. She could hear birds in the trees, the splash of water. She could smell fallen leaves and moss. She didn't think about anything else. Her body started to tingle slightly. She caught her breath. Was this it? Was she about to do magic? It would be so cool. What would she be able to do? The tingling feeling faded.

"Mia, stop thinking about it. Just let it happen," Bracken said.

Mia heard Sita give a gasp. "Oh, wow!"

Mia desperately wanted to open her eyes. What was Sita doing? Had she discovered what magic she could do?

Bracken stepped onto her knees. "Pet me, Mia. Don't think about anyone else. You need to lose yourself in the moment so the magic can come in."

Mia ran her hands down Bracken's fluffy coat. She concentrated on the feeling of his soft fur as she petted him, breathing in his warm scent. The tingling feeling started again, but this time, she didn't stop and think about it; she just relaxed. The tingling spread from her toes to her head. She felt like every part of her was waking up, opening like a flower in the sun. She felt linked to the whole world, joyful, alive….

"You've connected to the magic," Bracken said. "Open your eyes."

Mia opened her eyes. Everything looked sharper, as though she could see each blade of grass, every vein on every leaf, every hair on Bracken's russet-red body. She slowly looked around. Lexi was still sitting on the ground, her face screwed up in concentration. Juniper was sitting on her shoulder.

"You're trying too hard. Just relax," Mia heard him say.

Bracken bounded in front of her. "What do you feel?"

"Like I can see everything really clearly," breathed Mia.

"That could mean your magic abilities are to do with sight," said Bracken. "I think I know how to find out for sure." He bounded to the stream. "Take a rock out of the water."

As Mia looked into the stream, she gasped. She could see through the swirling eddies to the pebbles and rocks below, the little fish slipping through the weeds, the water beetles spinning around. "It's like I'm looking through a magnifying glass."

"With the power of sight, you'll be able to do much more than just see everything around you really clearly," said Bracken. "Look into

the surface of a wet rock and say the name of
someone you know."

Mia took a rock out of the water,
wondering what was going to happen. The
surface shone like a mirror. "Mom," she
whispered. She almost dropped the rock in
surprise as a faint picture appeared on the
wet surface. She could see a fuzzy image of
her mom in the kitchen at Grandma Anne's,
cleaning the cupboards.

"What do you see?" Bracken said.

"My mom. Look."

"I can't see it," he told her, shaking his head. "It's your magic that lets you see the image. As you practice more, you'll be able to use shiny surfaces to see what's happening elsewhere really clearly, and you'll be able to hear what's being said and look at the details of a scene. You'll also be able to see the past and glimpses of the future, and you might even learn to see into people's minds."

"Oh, wow!" said Mia, her thoughts racing. She glanced around and saw Sita touching a broken stem of Queen Anne's lace. As she ran her fingers along it, the stem strengthened and repaired until it was tall and strong again. "Look at that!" she said.

"Sita's abilities must have to do with healing," said Bracken.

Sita came over with Willow beside her. Her eyes were shining. "I feel amazing!" She took Mia's hands in hers and Mia immediately felt soothed, as if someone had wrapped a cozy blanket around her shoulders. "Willow thinks I'm going to learn how to comfort people and heal them," said Sita. "Can you do that, too?"

"No, my magic's different—it has to do with seeing things," said Mia.

Lexi cartwheeled through the clearing toward them, jumping to her feet after the fifth cartwheel. "Every part of me is bursting with energy. I want to run and jump and climb!"

"Then do it," urged Juniper, scampering up a tree. "Come on!"

Lexi shot up the tree trunk after him, as agile as a squirrel herself. They climbed high into the tree in just a few seconds. Straddling a branch, she wrapped her legs around it and hung down. "Look at me!" she cried, waving at them.

"Be careful!" exclaimed Sita.

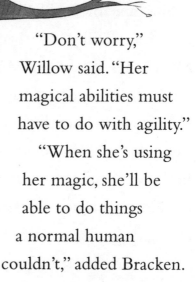

"Don't worry,"
Willow said. "Her
magical abilities must
have to do with agility."

"When she's using
her magic, she'll be
able to do things
a normal human
couldn't," added Bracken.

As if to prove his point,
Lexi pulled herself upward,climbed onto
the branch, and then jumped down to
the ground easily, turning a somersault
as she landed and springing lightly to
her feet.

"This is awesome!" she said, beaming.

"Now that you've connected with Star
Magic once, you'll find it much easier
next time," Juniper said. "If you practice,
you'll soon be able to use your magical

abilities in the blink of an eye. But now you should release the magic. It will tire you out if you use it for too long at first."

"How do we release it?" Sita asked.

"Imagine you're closing a door on it in your mind," said Bracken.

Shutting her eyes, Mia did as he said. The feeling of energy faded, and when she blinked her eyes open, the world was back to normal again. She felt slightly dizzy. She swayed and looked at the others—they looked slightly wobbly, too.

"We should practice every day," said Lexi.

Juniper jumped onto Lexi's shoulders. "You should all start using your abilities to help people. Even if it's just with small things. When you use magic to do good, the magic current will be strengthened, and your magic abilities will grow."

"What about dark magic?" said Mia, looking at Bracken. "What happens when people use that?"

Bracken's ears flattened. "Dark magic comes from the ground. Bad people can use it to conjure Shades—evil spirits who exist in the shadows. Once a Shade has been conjured, it can be released into the world to bring misery and unhappiness. It can also be trapped inside an object, like a necklace, book, or toy that the person using the dark magic will give to someone they want to harm in some way."

"How can a Shade harm someone?" said Lexi.

Juniper swung onto Lexi's other shoulder. "Some Shades whisper to people, encouraging their worst feelings of jealousy, anger, and greed, twisting their minds. Other Shades bring nightmares to life or trap people using magic or cause accidents to happen. There are many different types. If we find a Shade trapped in an object, we must release it and send it back to the shadows."

"But only a Spirit Speaker can do that," Bracken put in.

"What's a Spirit Speaker?" asked Sita curiously.

"Some Star Friends are called Spirit Speakers because they have the magic ability to command spirits. But none of you seems to have that ability," Bracken answered. "If we find an object with a Shade trapped in it, we'll just have to hide it where no one else will ever find it."

"And stop the person who conjured the Shade in the first place," added Juniper.

Willow shivered. "We'll have to be careful. If someone is using dark magic, it could be very dangerous."

"I don't care," said Mia determinedly. "I'm not scared."

"Me neither," said Lexi.

"So, how do we find out if someone is using dark magic?" Sita asked.

"We need to watch for strange things happening, people acting in unusual ways, or people being exceptionally unhappy, miserable, hurtful, or scared," Bracken said.

"I think the older Star Animals are right and someone is using dark magic," said Willow. "As soon as we got here, I could smell it in the air—a hint of sourness that wafts in and out. It makes the hairs on my back prickle."

"What about you, Bracken?" asked Mia. "Can you smell dark magic, too?"

He shook his head. "Not all Star Animals can. It's a bit like different humans having different magical abilities. Willow is sensitive to dark magic and can smell it. I can't."

"Sorrel—the wildcat—is even more sensitive than I am," said Willow. "I am able to smell a hint of dark magic in the air, but she is able to follow the scent of it."

"Will she help us?" asked Lexi eagerly.

"No," said Willow. "She'll be traveling to find

her own Star Friend."

"We don't need her anyway," declared Bracken. "We'll be fine on our own."

Mia nodded. "We'd better keep our eyes and ears open for anything weird going on," she said, looking at Lexi and Sita, who both nodded.

"And in the meantime, we should keep learning to use our magic," said Lexi.

"This is all so amazing!" said Sita, petting Willow. "I can hardly believe it."

Mia crouched down and hugged Bracken. Sita was right. It *was* amazing! In twenty-four hours, everything had changed. She didn't know where it was all going to lead, but one thing was for sure—their lives were never going to be the same again!

8

WORKING TOGETHER

When Mia got home, she went right up to her room. She wanted some time on her own to think about everything that had happened. As she reached the top of the stairs, Cleo came out of her bedroom.

"Do you think I'm pretty?" Cleo asked.

Mia was taken aback. "What?"

"Do you think I'm pretty?" Cleo demanded.

"Um … yes," said Mia.

"Not as beautiful as Beth, though?" Cleo persisted.

"Well ... Beth is really, really pretty," said Mia, thinking of Cleo's friend with her waist-length dark hair and olive skin. "Like stunningly, model-looking pretty."

Cleo frowned and pulled the compact out of her pocket to look at her reflection. "It's not fair," she grumbled. "Why should Beth be so perfect? Why should she be the one who gets to be a model?"

Mia edged past her. Cleo was so busy looking in the mirror that she didn't seem to notice.

"Okay, and today's prize for the weirdest sister goes to Cleo Greene," Mia muttered as she reached her room.

Shutting the door after her, she sank down

on her bed. Alone at last.

Mia remembered what Bracken had told her as she had left the clearing. He had said that now that she was his Star Friend, he would always appear if she called his name. She decided to try it. "Bracken?" she whispered.

There was a shimmer of starlight and then Bracken appeared, his ears pricked, his tail waving.

"Hello!" he said, leaping onto the bed.

She hugged him, burying her face in his soft fur.

As he nuzzled her neck, she felt a wave of happiness sweep over her.

"So, did you like doing magic today?" he asked.

"Definitely!" she said. "It's wonderful that Lexi and Sita are Star Friends, too." She rubbed his back. "Are there any others around here? Or is it just us?"

"Just you," said Bracken.

"Are you sure?" Mia remembered what she had been thinking about the night before. "It's just that there's this elderly lady I know—Aunt Carol—she was friends with my grandma, who died last month. I was wondering if she might be a Star Friend and … well … if my grandma might have been one. Grandma Anne definitely believed in magic, and she was always helping people."

Bracken looked puzzled. "There are definitely no other Star Animals anywhere near here— only the ones I traveled with. We would have sensed any others when we arrived. The elderly lady you're friends with can't be a Star Friend."

"Oh," said Mia, disappointed.

"Maybe she's the kind of person who could have been a Star Friend but never met a Star Animal," Bracken suggested. "That sometimes happens. However, your grandma might have been a Star Friend. When she died, her Star Animal would have returned to the Star World." He nuzzled her. "I can't say if she was or not, but I'm sure that if your grandma was a Star Friend, she'd be really happy to know that you are one, too, Mia."

She hugged him tightly, and an image of Grandma Anne's smiling face filled her mind.

Bracken licked her hands and Mia felt a new determination steal over her.

I'll do my best to be a good Star Friend, she told

Grandma Anne in her head. *I promise I'll make you proud.*

It was very hard waiting for afternoon to come the next day. Mia longed to go to the clearing and start practicing magic again, but Lexi was busy with activities all morning, and Sita was out with her family. The day seemed to crawl by, but finally it was three o'clock, and Lexi and Sita arrived at Mia's house on their bikes. They set off to the clearing right away.

As they turned on to the road that led to Grandma Anne's, they passed Violet playing in her yard with her two rabbits. She looked up, but they didn't stop. Mia felt a pang of guilt as they rode past. But she couldn't stop and say hi; she and the others wouldn't be able to do magic if Violet joined them.

Riding down the road, they left their bikes in Grandma Anne's yard and pushed their way down the overgrown path. As soon as they ran into the clearing, Bracken, Willow, and Juniper each appeared out of thin air. Juniper scampered up Lexi's arm and jumped onto her head, making her giggle. Willow danced around Sita and then butted her gently with her head, and Bracken bounced around doing play bows and barking. They seemed as happy as the girls to all be together.

"Let's do more magic," Mia suggested, shooting a look at Lexi and Sita. They both nodded eagerly and sat down on the grass with their animals beside them. Mia breathed in and out, opening her mind, letting all her thoughts fade away. She felt the tingling start, and magic flowed into her. Opening her eyes, she saw everything with super sharpness again.

Sita and Lexi were already on their feet.

Lexi turned two front flips effortlessly. "I feel incredible!"

Sita smiled happily. "It's the best feeling. I just

want to go and help people."

"Me, too. I wish…." Mia broke off. She felt as if her eyes were being drawn toward a patch of brambles at the edge of the clearing. She frowned. Why did she feel she needed to look at that spot?

"What is it, Mia?" Sita asked.

"Shh." Mia held up a hand. She could tell that something was wrong, something needed help. She looked into the bushes and concentrated hard. Normally she'd only be able to see a cluster of bushes, but now she could see *through* the branches. There was an animal there—a young squirrel caught in the thorns. It was struggling, but it couldn't get free.

"Over there," said Mia, pointing. "There's a squirrel who needs help."

They all followed her to the patch of thick brambles. Now that they were closer, they could see the branches moving. Not caring about the thorns that caught at her skin, Mia pulled the

branches apart. "Look!" The little gray squirrel
froze for a moment and then struggled harder,
getting even more tangled up.

"You can help it," said
Bracken. "Work together."

"Sita," said Willow.
"Use your magic to
calm it first."

Crouching down,
Sita reached into
the branches. As she
whispered to the squirrel, it
stopped struggling. She touched
it, and all the little animal's tension and fear
seemed to drain away. It stared at her with
trusting dark eyes. She gently untangled the
thorns from its fur and lifted the squirrel out.

"You poor thing," she soothed, petting its
coat and letting it nestle against her.

"That could be its drey up there," said Mia,
spotting a nest made of leaves and twigs, high

up in a fork in one of the branches.

Juniper scampered up the tree and inspected the drey. "Yes, this is where it lives," he called. "Lexi, can you bring it up? Then it can recover in safety."

Lexi took the squirrel from Sita. Mia wondered if it would start to panic again, but it seemed to accept them as friends now. Lexi tucked it into her coat and started to climb the tree. As she did so, Mia blinked. Her eyes felt weird. It was as if she could see where Lexi would climb a second before she did it.

"Bracken! I can see what she's going to do before she does it," she whispered.

"It must be part of your magical ability," Bracken said. "You can probably choose to use it or not. Try and control it with your mind."

I want to see normally! thought Mia. It was too weird seeing a second in advance.

To her relief, her eyes returned to seeing things in normal time, although she could still feel Star Magic tingling through her.

Lexi reached the fork in the tree and placed the squirrel inside its nest. Juniper chattered at it, and it chattered back. Then Lexi and Juniper climbed down the tree. Lexi jumped the last few feet. "It's safe up there," she said.

They all exchanged happy smiles.

"That was fun," said Sita. "I want to help something else." She glanced at Mia's hands. "Maybe I can heal your hands."

Mia had been so busy thinking about the squirrel that she hadn't noticed her hands hurting. Looking down, she saw that they were covered in scratches. She held them out.

Sita touched them. Mia felt a soothing warmth and the scratches stopped bleeding, but they didn't disappear completely.

Sita looked disappointed. "I can't seem to help more than that."

"Don't worry," said Willow. "I'm sure if you

keep using your magic, you'll be able to soon."
Suddenly she tensed, her large ears swiveling.
"Someone's coming!"

The Star Animals vanished just as Violet
appeared in the clearing.

"Hi," said Sita, smiling at her.

"What are *you* doing here?" Lexi said.

Violet raised her eyebrows. "I live near here.
What's your excuse? I've seen you coming
here every day." She gave them a curious look.
"Why?"

"It's none of your business," said Lexi.

"We just like it here," said Sita.

"We're going now, anyway," said Mia.

"You don't have to," Violet said quickly. "You can stay if you want."

"Um … actually, we'd better go," said Mia, feeling awkward. "Mom will be wondering where we are."

"Okay. Whatever," Violet said, shrugging and scuffing her foot on the ground. "'Bye."

Mia, Lexi, and Sita headed for the path. As they were about to leave the clearing, Mia glanced back. Violet was watching them go with an almost wistful expression on her face. Mia suddenly felt bad and took a step back toward her, but Violet turned away quickly and hurried into the trees.

9
HELPING OUT

"Morning," Mia's mom and dad said when
Mia went downstairs for breakfast the next day.
She'd slept well with Bracken curled up at her
feet. He'd promised he would vanish if anyone
came in, but he hadn't had to, and it had been
wonderful to wake up and cuddle him.

"Hi." Mia poured herself some cereal. She
waved at Alex, who was in his high chair. He
pulled his dirty bib up over his face, peeking
out from behind it.

"Alex, don't do that—you'll get oatmeal in

your hair," her dad said, pulling the bib down so he could spoon some oatmeal into Alex's mouth. Alex took a mouthful but then blew a raspberry so that it all splattered all over Dad. "Alex!" he groaned.

Mia handed him a cloth. "Now you've got oatmeal in *your* hair!" Mealtimes were always messy when Alex was involved. Keeping a safe distance from the high chair, she sat down with her own cereal.

"What time are Lexi and Sita coming over?" her mom asked.

"Nine thirty," said Mia. "We're going to finish the posters for our bake sale and put them up around town so everyone knows about it." *And after that, we'll ride our bikes to the woods and practice doing magic again*, she added to herself, her heart racing at the thought.

"Okay, well, I'm dropping Cleo off at Beth's for an hour or so while I take Alex on a play date, but Dad will be here if you need him. If you go

out, tell him where you're going." Her mom
went to the door. "Cleo! You need to have some
breakfast before I bring you to Beth's."

A few minutes later, Cleo came downstairs
in her pajamas and robe. Her hair was
disheveled, and there were faint gray shadows
under her eyes.

"Ce-o!" Alex crowed. It was his way of
saying her name.

Cleo ignored him. Mia frowned in surprise.
Usually Cleo made a big fuss of their little
brother. But now she just pulled out a chair
and slumped into it.

"Toast?" her mom said, handing Cleo a plate. "You'd better get a move on—we've got to leave in fifteen minutes."

"I can't be ready by then!" Cleo pulled the compact out of her robe pocket and checked her reflection. "I look awful. I need at least half an hour."

"You're only going to Beth's house. Give your hair a quick brush and you'll be fine," Mom said.

"But I have to do my makeup! Beth always looks great." Cleo looked at herself from different angles in the compact and examined a small spot on her chin. "It's not fair," she muttered. "Beth never gets spots. Why does she get to be so perfect?"

Mia looked at her in surprise. She was used to Cleo laughing about how annoying it was to have a beautiful best friend like Beth, but today she sounded genuinely resentful.

"Cleo! Put that mirror away and eat your

breakfast!" said Mom, scooping the compact out of Cleo's hands and putting it on the table. Cleo grabbed it and stuffed it in her pocket. She sat munching her toast, not saying another word.

"Teenagers!" Mia saw her dad mouth silently at her mom.

Mia finished her cereal. "I'm going to get dressed."

"Will it take you half an hour to get ready, Mia?" her dad asked with a grin as he cleared away the remains of Alex's oatmeal.

She grinned back at him. "Oh, at least."

Knowing she was being teased, Cleo scowled at them both and stomped back to her room.

Dad shook his head pityingly. "It's hard being fifteen," he said.

"I heard that!" Cleo shouted down the stairs.

As soon as Sita and Lexi arrived, they raced up to Mia's room. They were going to finish the posters with the door shut so Bracken, Juniper, and Willow could appear.

"I used my magic last night," Sita said excitedly as Mia closed the door and the three Star Animals appeared.

"What did you do?" Mia asked as Bracken bounded around her legs.

"Arjun was crying, and Mom couldn't calm him down." Arjun was Sita's baby brother. "When Mom went out of the room, I used my magic. I sensed he had a tummy ache. I put my hands on his tummy and felt the pain fade away. And then he stopped crying and went to sleep. Mom was really happy."

"That's so awesome!" said Mia.

"It felt incredible," said Sita, her eyes shining.

Willow nuzzled her hands. "You're going to be an amazing healer, Sita. I know you are."

"I did something, too," said Lexi, petting

Juniper. "The little boy next door had been playing with his model airplane. It got stuck on the garage roof, and I heard him crying. When he went inside for lunch, I checked to make sure that there was no one watching and used my magic to climb up a drainpipe and get it. He was really surprised when he came out after lunch and found it on the ground. His mom said the wind must have blown it down." She grinned. "But it wasn't the wind—it was me!"

"Cool!" said Mia, wishing she had a story to tell, too. "I didn't do anything magical. Bracken and I just talked. I'll have to try and find something to do today." She grinned at the others. "I can't have you both doing magic and me not."

"Are we going to go to the clearing?" Juniper asked. "I like it there. It's a good place for playing and practicing magic."

"It is," agreed Willow. "The air smells sweet because there's a lot of Star Magic there."

"We can go in a little while—but first we've got to finish making posters," Lexi said. "The bake sale is on Saturday, four days from today. We need to get some posters up so that people know about our stand and what we're raising money for. That way, people will buy tons of cupcakes."

Mia got out the posterboard. "We'd better get started then."

When the posters were finished, the girls set off around town on their bikes to put them up. Their first stop was the village hall where, to their surprise, they found Violet standing by the bulletin board.

"Hi," said Sita as they got off their bikes.

Violet smiled back. "Hi."

"Are you putting up a flyer, too?" Mia asked her.

"Yes, I'm organizing a decorate-a-cookie table to help endangered animals at the Harvest Show," said Violet. "You should come along." She looked at them. They were all staring at her. "What?" she said.

"But … but we're doing that!" Mia burst out. "Well, we're organizing a bake sale, and that's pretty much the same thing."

"You stole our idea!" Lexi said.

Violet's eyebrows shot up. "I so didn't!"

"You must have!" exclaimed Lexi. "You must have been spying on us!"

"Seriously? You're not that interesting, and I've got better things to do with my time than spy on you!" Violet snapped.

"It's obvious there's just been a mix-up," said Sita. "It's funny in a way—I mean, both you and Mia having the same idea." She looked around hopefully, but none of the others smiled back at her. "Why don't we all do a table together?" she continued. "Violet could have one end of the table for decorating her cookies, and we could sell cupcakes at the other end. After all, we're raising money for the same cause, so it's a little crazy to have two tables. We'll probably raise more if we join forces."

Lexi glanced at Mia.

"All right," Mia muttered. "You can share

with us, Violet."

"Thanks." Violet rolled her eyes. "But no."

"What?" Mia frowned.

Violet gave her a haughty look. "I know you all might find this impossible to believe, but I don't want to have a table with you. I'd rather do my own thing."

"Violet, that's silly…," Sita began.

Violet shrugged. "Well, it's what I'm going to do." She stalked off.

"She's *so* annoying!" Lexi burst out.

Sita sighed. "To be fair, we didn't make it sound like we really wanted her to share with us. I don't blame her for saying no."

Mia felt a flicker of guilt.

Lexi put her arm through Mia's. "Come on—let's put up the rest of the posters and then go to the clearing. I want to do some more magic!"

A smile caught at Mia's lips. "Me, too," she said.

10
PRACTICING MAGIC

"That was even easier than yesterday!" Mia said, opening her eyes and looking around at the clearing as she let Star Magic flow into her.

Bracken wagged his tail. "I told you it would get easier every time."

Sita came over with Willow. "My magic feels much stronger today. Can I try again to heal those scratches on your hands?"

Mia held out her hands. Sita touched the scratches and shut her eyes, breathing deeply. Mia felt warmth flood over her skin, and the scratches tingled. She gasped as they started to shrink and fade, then vanish completely.

"Sita! Look!"

"I did it!" Sita said in delight.

Mia turned to Bracken, even more eager to do something herself. "What should I try?"

"Why don't you work on using your sight to find out what's happening elsewhere?" he said. "If you practice, you should be able to hear what's being said. You might be able to find out if anyone needs help. You just need something that reflects light to look into."

"I should have kept that compact I gave Cleo," Mia said. "I could have used the mirror in that."

She took another rock out of the river and sat down on a tree stump, holding it in her hands.

"Think about something or someone you really want to see," said Bracken.

Mia thought about Cleo. She let the magic

flow from her into the rock she was holding.
An image appeared in the shining surface. It
was a fuzzy picture of Cleo in her bedroom.

"Can you see anything?" Bracken asked.

Mia nodded. "Yes, I can see Cleo. But it's not
very clear."

"Try to relax and just let the magic flow,"
suggested Bracken.

Mia breathed slowly in and out. "It's
working," she said as the image came into
focus. Cleo was sitting at her desk, the compact
in her hand. She seemed to be talking to
someone but there was no one there. Mia
frowned. Maybe her phone was on speaker?

Mia heard a faint buzz and then, little by little, she began to make out what Cleo was saying.

"You're right, it's really not fair," Cleo was muttering angrily. "Why should the good things always happen to her? What about me?" Mia watched as her sister brought the compact closer to her face. "You understand, don't you?" she said to the mirror.

Mia stared. Cleo was talking to her reflection! That was seriously odd. She blinked and let the vision fade.

"What did you see?" Bracken asked.

"Cleo was being really weird," said Mia.

Bracken pricked his ears hopefully. "If she's unhappy in some way, maybe you can use magic to help her."

"I'm not sure how," said Mia. "It sounds like she's mad at her best friend Beth for being so pretty. Maybe I should try and see if I can find someone else who has a problem."

Bracken nodded, and Mia used the rock to see her mom. An image appeared showing her searching for her purse with Mia's dad.

"Where did you have it last?" her dad was asking.

"At the gas station," her mom said. "But I called them, and they said they haven't found it. If I don't find it soon, I'll have to cancel all my credit cards."

Mia had an idea. "Mom's purse," she said to the rock.

The image rippled and changed to show her mom's purse. It had been pushed under the bookcase in the living room—probably by Alex. Mia pulled out her phone and texted her mom.

Hi Mom. Just remembered—I meant to tell you, I saw Alex playing with your purse in the living room, near the bookcase. M xx

She said her mom's name and watched in the rock as her mom checked the text, then hurried to the bookcase. Her face lit up as she pulled the purse out from underneath it. "It's here!" she called to Mia's dad. She took out her phone.

A few seconds later, Mia's phone beeped with a text.

Thank you! Just found it! Phew! X

Mia smiled. Okay, it had only been a small thing, but it had definitely been a good deed. She let the vision fade.

"So? What happened?" Bracken said.

When Mia told him, he jumped around her, his tail waving.

Mia grinned. "I know what magic I want to practice next," she said. "That weird thing I did the other day where I can see where people are going to move before they actually do."

"Try with me!" said Bracken. "Use your magic to see which way I'm going to go and try and tag me!"

He stood in front of her, poised and ready.

Mia concentrated on letting the strange feeling creep into her eyes. She nodded at him. "Left!" she shouted, a fraction of a second before he actually moved. She sprang to the left at the same time, reaching out with her hand and touching his soft fur.

Bracken rolled on to his tummy and jumped to his feet. "That was good! Try again."

This time she tagged him as he sprang to the right.

"What are you doing?" Lexi asked.

Mia explained.

"Let's all play!" said Lexi.

Soon Mia was chasing everyone. It was

much more fun being
It in a game of tag
if you could see
where people
were going to go!
She tagged Sita,
Bracken, Willow,
and Juniper easily.
The only person
who managed
to get away from
her was Lexi, and that
was only because she could
move so fast. Mia chased her around
the clearing, changing direction a split second
before Lexi did each time but never quite
managing to tag her with her outstretched
hand. Lexi was faster than a cheetah!

In the end, they stopped and fell on the
grass together.

"That was fun!" said Lexi, her eyes shining.

Mia laughed and stretched out her arms above her head.

"Well, I'm definitely never playing tag with either of you again!" Sita said with a grin.

"I guess we'd better go home," said Mia, sitting up reluctantly.

"When we meet up next, we should try and think up a plan to find out if dark magic is being used nearby," said Sita, glancing at Willow. "Willow says she feels sure that something is going on."

Willow pawed at the grass uneasily. "I keep getting a scent of dark magic, but I can't figure out exactly where it's coming from."

Bracken pricked his ears. "Maybe we can all figure it out over the next few days."

Sita, Mia, and Lexi got back to Mia's house just as Lexi's mom arrived.

"Did you have fun?" Lexi's mom asked,

helping her put the bike in the trunk of the car.

"Yep!" said Lexi, winking at the others. "Lots and lots!"

Sita said good-bye and rode off. Mia waved to Lexi and then went inside. Cleo was in the hall.

Mia looked at her closely, remembering how weirdly she'd been behaving when she'd watched her in the rock. "Hi," she said.

"Hi," Cleo muttered.

"Are you okay?" Mia said.

"Yes. Well, I mean obviously I'm not as pretty as Beth in your eyes and obviously I shouldn't be a model like Beth should," she said. "But aside from that, I'm just fine." She stalked into the living room.

Mia stared after her and then went into the kitchen. Her mom was helping Alex paint a picture.

"Mom," Mia said. "Do you think Cleo's acting a little weird?"

"In what way?' her mom said.

"I don't know," said Mia. "It's just that she keeps saying stuff about not being as pretty as Beth."

"Oh, that's just Cleo being fifteen," her mom said, turning her attention back to Alex. "Paint the paper, Alex, not your hands. At that age you have days when life doesn't seem fair and it feels like no one understands you. Don't worry about it. She'll get over it in a day or two."

Mia bit her lip.

Her mom glanced up, saw her worried face, and gave her a quick smile. "It's sweet of you to be concerned, but really, she's fine, Mia."

"Okay." Mia sighed, hoping her mom was right.

11
TROUBLE!

Over the next few days, Cleo didn't become her normal teasing, gossiping, cheerful self again. If anything, she became even more grumpy and lost in her own thoughts. If she did speak to Mia, it was only to snap at her.

Most of the time Mia was too busy practicing magic or talking to Bracken to think about it much. But on Thursday evening, Mia knocked on Cleo's bedroom door to make sure she'd remembered her offer to make chocolate brownies for the bake sale on Saturday.

No one answered but the door was ajar, so Mia pushed it open and looked inside. Cleo wasn't there. Mia's gaze was caught by a glint of light. The compact was on the desk, its lid open. As she looked at it, Mia felt a sudden strange urge to pick it up.

She walked into the room and reached for it.

"What are you doing?" Cleo's voice snapped. Mia swung around. Cleo was standing in the doorway. She strode over and grabbed the compact. "That's mine!"

Mia recoiled in shock as Cleo stepped forward threateningly. "Get out of my room!" she yelled.

"I'm sorry!" Mia ran out. The door slammed shut after her.

Mia turned and stared at the door, her heart pounding. Okay, Cleo didn't like her going into her room, but she'd never screamed at her like that before. Something very, very weird was going on. This wasn't Cleo just being fifteen and moody.

She hurried back to her room. "Bracken!" she whispered.

Bracken instantly appeared and bounded up to her. "Are we going to do something? Should we try practicing your magic again?" He stopped, tipping his head to one side. "Are you all right, Mia? You seem upset."

"Mmm," she said distractedly.

He stood on his back legs and put his paws on her knees. "What's the matter? You can tell me."

She hugged him. "I'm worried about Cleo. She's acting so strangely. I just went to her room, and she was really odd."

"Why don't you use your magic to see what she's doing now?" Bracken said.

Mia went over to her bedroom mirror. Taking a deep breath, she opened herself to the current of magic. "Cleo," she whispered. The mirror shimmered, and then an image of Cleo appeared in the glass. She was sitting on her bed, talking to something in her hand. At first Mia thought it was her phone but then, as the vision got clearer, she realized that it was the compact again.

"I hate her," Cleo was muttering to the compact. "You're right, I should do something about it. She deserves it."

A chill ran down Mia's spine. "She's talking to herself in the mirror again and saying really weird stuff," she said.

Bracken flattened his ears. "In a mirror? Oh, no, no, no. Mia, this isn't good. Which mirror?"

Mia frowned. Why did that matter? "It's the make-up compact that used to be Grandma Anne's. Mom said I could have it, but I gave it to Cleo a few days ago."

"About the time when she started behaving strangely?" Bracken asked. "Mia, we've been looking for evidence of dark magic—well, that mirror could have a Shade trapped inside it. Mirror Shades can work all sorts of evil. They manipulate anyone who looks into the mirror. They pretend to be that person's friend, but then they start twisting their minds, making them jealous and angry."

Mia's heart felt like it was in her throat. "Then what happens?"

"If the Shade isn't stopped, the person can end up doing awful things."

Mia frowned. "But Bracken, the compact was Grandma Anne's. How can it have something evil in it? Grandma Anne would never have something evil in the house."

"If she was a Star Friend, she might have tried to hide it to make sure that no one else would use it," Bracken said.

Mia swallowed. It made horrible sense.

"We've got to get the mirror away from Cleo. But it won't be easy," she said, thinking about how angry Cleo had been when she had found Mia near the compact in her room. "What should we do?"

"I think we should contact the others and come up with a plan together," said Bracken.

Mia nodded. "It's too late for them to come over now, but they're coming over tomorrow and spending the night, so we can figure out what to do then." She sank down on her bed. Bracken jumped up beside her, and she pulled him onto her lap. "Oh, Bracken, Cleo is going to be okay, isn't she?"

"I hope so," he said. "I really do."

Mia's dreams that night were full of dark, shadowy figures hiding in mirrors and mocking her. She woke up feeling sick with worry. Was there really a Shade in Cleo's compact?

Was that why her sister had been acting so strange and scary? Even cuddling Bracken didn't help her feel better. She just wanted to rush into her sister's room and grab the compact, but even she could see that wasn't a good idea.

As soon as the others arrived, she took them upstairs. Bracken, Juniper, and Willow appeared almost instantly.

"What's the matter?' said Sita, seeing Mia's face.

Mia told everyone about the compact.

Willow sniffed at the air, and her ears flickered anxiously. "Bracken's right. I can smell the sour scent of dark magic here."

"What are we going to do?" Juniper ran along Mia's bed and jumped onto the back of her chair. "If it is a Shade, we should send it back to the shadows. But because none of you is a Spirit Speaker, we can't do that."

"We need another plan, then," said Lexi.

"The next best thing is to steal the compact and put it where no one will ever find it," said Juniper.

"Like Grandma Anne tried to," said Mia.

"When Cleo leaves her room, I could sneak in and get it," said Lexi. "I'll use my magic to move really fast."

But Cleo's door stayed firmly shut. In the end, they went downstairs to start making the cupcakes.

"Lunchtime!' Mom called up to Cleo when the cupcakes were cooling on wire racks.

"She'll have to come out now," Mia whispered to the others.

Cleo came downstairs, but Mia saw the shape of the compact in the pocket of her jeans. Now what were they going to do?

Cleo hardly said a word at lunch. When Mia asked her when she was going to make the chocolate brownies, she shrugged and didn't give an answer. As soon as she could, she went back upstairs and shut her door. Mia thought about various possibilities while she, Lexi, and Sita iced and decorated the cupcakes. How could they get a hold of the compact? How could they get Cleo out of her room?

At six o'clock, her mom served lasagna and salad, and Cleo finally emerged from her room again.

"Aren't you and Dad having dinner with us?" Mia said when her mom didn't sit down.

"No, we're going to stop next door for an hour or so. We'll take Alex with us. Cleo, you're in charge of everyone else while we're out."

Cleo hunched over her plate, pushing the food around with her fork.

"Okay, Cleo?" Mom said.

"Mmm," Cleo muttered.

Mom smiled at the rest of them. "If you need us, just give us a call."

Once Mom and Dad had left with Alex, Cleo took the compact out of her pocket and began to open it up. Mia, Lexi, and Sita exchanged glances.

"That's nice. Can I see it?" Lexi asked, reaching out.

"No!" Cleo snapped, pulling the compact away and shutting it quickly.

They continued eating in an uncomfortable

silence. They had just finished when the doorbell rang.

Mia jumped up, glad of an excuse to escape the tension at the dinner table. "I'll get it."

She went to the door. Beth was standing on the doorstep. "Hi, is Cleo here?" she asked.

"Yeah," said Mia. "Come in."

Beth followed her inside. Cleo was in the kitchen doorway. She scowled when she saw Beth. "What do you want?"

Beth blinked in surprise. "I … I just thought I'd come over to see you. You've been really weird the last few days. Are you okay?"

Cleo glared at her. "Like you'd care."

Confusion crossed Beth's face. "What do you mean?"

"Oh, don't act like you don't know. All you care about is yourself." Cleo's face creased in an ugly sneer. "I'm Beth, the model. I'm Beth and I'm so beautiful. No one else matters."

"What are you talking about?" Beth asked.

"You think you're so perfect, don't you?"
Cleo said angrily. "Well, no one else thinks so,
and no one likes you, and soon—very soon—
you'll be sorry!"

"Cleo!" Mia burst out, seeing the shocked
look on Beth's face.

"I'm not listening to this," Beth said, her
eyes filling with tears. "I don't know what's up
with you."

Beth turned and ran out of the house, and Cleo marched upstairs.

"Beth! Wait!" called Mia, but Beth didn't stop.

Lexi and Sita hurried out of the kitchen. They had obviously heard every word of the argument.

"What do we do now?" said Lexi.

"We have to get that compact," said Mia.

"Maybe I could get it when she goes to sleep," said Lexi.

"We can't wait until then." Mia thought for a moment and then nodded. "Okay, how about this for a plan…."

12

SHOWDOWN WITH
THE SHADE

Ten minutes later, Sita stood outside Cleo's
bedroom door with a mug of hot chocolate
decorated with whipped cream and tiny
marshmallows. Mia was in her bedroom, using
her magic to watch in her bedroom mirror,
and Lexi was in the yard below with Juniper.

Bracken nuzzled Mia's hands. She rubbed
his head gratefully as she heard Sita knock on
Cleo's door. Would the plan work? The first
part of it depended on Sita's ability to get Cleo
out of her room.

"Cleo, it's Sita," Sita called softly. "I've brought you some hot chocolate."

The door opened. Cleo gave Sita a suspicious look. "Where's Mia?"

"With Lexi," Sita said. "Are you okay?"

She handed Cleo the hot chocolate. As Cleo took it, Sita's hand closed gently on her arm. "You seemed really upset earlier," she said, her voice sympathetic.

Cleo's frown began to fade as Sita touched her.

"I have been feeling odd," she admitted slowly. "I don't know what's been the matter with me this week."

"Why don't you come downstairs with me and talk about it?" said Sita gently. "Simi, my big sister, says I'm a good listener. I'd like to listen to you."

Mia held her breath, hoping Sita's persuasive, calming magic would work and that Cleo would go with her.

To her relief, Cleo nodded. "Okay, but don't go in my room." She shut the door firmly. "I'll hear if anyone opens the door," she warned.

"No one will open your door," Sita promised. She led Cleo downstairs, shooting a quick look over her shoulder and winking.

Mia ran to her window. "Lexi!" she hissed into the dusky yard. The next part of the plan involved Lexi getting the compact—without using the bedroom door, just in case Cleo decided to check.

"On it!" Lexi whispered back. Mia watched as she grabbed hold of the Virginia creeper that covered the house and pulled herself easily up the wall. Juniper scampered beside her and stopped by the window. It was just slightly ajar. Lexi pulled it open, and then Juniper leaped inside. Lexi followed him.

"Time to go, Bracken," Mia said. She and Bracken ran as quietly as they could through the hallway and down the stairs. She paused on the bottom step. She could hear Sita talking soothingly to Cleo in the living room. "It must be awful to feel like that. You look so tired. Why don't you take a nap?"

Cleo yawned. "Now that you mention it, I do feel tired."

"I'll shut the curtains," said Sita. "And then you can take a little nap. I'll make sure everything is okay."

Mia slipped past the living-room doorway and ran into the kitchen. The French windows were open, and she could see Lexi outside.

"Got it!" Lexi hissed, holding up the compact. Juniper was on her shoulder.

Mia took the compact from Lexi. Her heart was pounding. "Should I open it?" She looked at Bracken.

"We do need to find out if there's a Shade in there," he said. "But be careful, Mia."

"Really, really careful," said Sita anxiously as she came out through the French windows. "Cleo's asleep now."

Mia opened the compact and looked into the mirror. As she did so, she caught sight of a shadowy gray shape flickering deep in the glass. The image grew clearer, becoming the reflection of a handsome boy with tousled blond hair and dark eyes.

"*What have we here?*" a voice said in her head. "*Not my Cleo, but someone else. A Star Friend for me to have fun with!*"

Mia felt anger surge through her. "Cleo's not your Cleo and yes, I'm a Star Friend, but you're not going to do anything with me."

"*Really?*" The Shade's voice was like golden syrup, smooth and tempting. His eyes looked deep into hers, kind and understanding. "*Don't you want to be special, Mia? Being the middle child must be hard. Your parents adore little Alex and his funny ways, and Cleo's the oldest, the firstborn. She'll always be the one they love most. That leaves you…. Well, where does it leave you?*"

His hypnotic voice wove its way into Mia's mind. He was right. She was just the middle one. Her parents did love Alex and Cleo more….

"Mia!" Bracken said. "Don't listen to the Shade. Use your magic to fight it."

With effort, Mia connected to the magic

current. As magic flowed into her, she looked at the Shade—really looked at it. The handsome face and sympathetic brown eyes melted away under her gaze, becoming a gray skull with glittering red eyes. The spell it was casting was broken. "No!" she cried. Repulsed, she threw the compact down.

The mirror smashed as it hit the ground. Juniper chattered and Willow bleated in alarm. Gray smoke started to seep out through the cracks in the broken glass.

"What's happening?" cried Lexi.

Bracken jumped in front of Mia as the smoke swirled together and formed a very tall, thin figure with gray skin, a skull-like face, and ragged clothes. The figure's slanted eyes glowed red in his bony face. Seeing the horror on the girls' faces, he laughed and stepped toward them.

"Finally, I am free!" He cracked his long bony fingers, then pointed at Mia. "Thank you, my dear. I never imagined you'd give me my freedom. You really have a lot to learn." He rubbed his hands together. "Now I can roam where I like, inhabit any mirror I like, cause whatever mischief I like."

"No!" she said bravely. "I won't let you."

The Shade laughed. "And how do you plan on stopping me? I see three Star Friends here, but not one of you is a Spirit Speaker." He spread his fingers. Sharp nails popped out like knives.

"What should we do?" Sita gasped.

The Shade stepped toward them.

Bracken growled. "Stay back!" Darting forward, he grabbed the Shade's leg with his teeth.

At the same moment, Willow charged and butted the Shade. Juniper leaped onto his head.

"No!" the Shade hissed, swiping at them with his long nails.

He caught Bracken's side, making the fox yelp.

"Bracken!" cried Mia. She threw herself at the Shade. He stood his ground and, as she hit his chest, he threw her backward as easily as if she weighed no more than a piece of paper. She landed on her back on the ground with a thump. The next moment the Shade was looming over her, laughing and showing off his teeth. "You think *you* can attack *me*?"

"Mia! Use your sight!" Bracken said.

She saw the Shade swipe down with his left

hand a second before he actually made the move. She rolled to the right and jumped to her feet just as Sita threw a flowerpot at him.

"Get off her!" Sita shouted. It hit his side, making him stagger.

Lexi grabbed a second flowerpot from the patio and charged at the Shade, using her super-speed to dodge his hands with ease. She hit him on the head. "Got you!" she gasped as he fell to the ground.

The Shade slowly sat up. Bracken growled warningly at him, Juniper chattered, and Willow lowered her head as if she was about to charge again.

Mia heard his silky smooth voice. "*Well, aren't you all very clever?*" he said. "*Really very clever indeed…. But who is the most clever? Who is going to be the* best *Star Friend? Who will be able to do the* most *magic? Don't try and tell me you haven't thought about that! Will it be you, Sita? Or you, Mia? Or you, Lexi? Don't you all*" *secretly wish you could be the best? One of you will be more powerful than all the others. I can see that. But who will it be?*" His voice weaved its way around their thoughts. Mia found she couldn't stop listening to it. She stared at him, aware the others were staring, too.

"You should all just sit down and let me slip away," said the Shade. "Then you can figure out between you who is the strongest, while I find more mirrors to inhabit, more people to enchant."

No, Mia wanted to say, but she couldn't get the word out. Instead, she found herself starting to nod in agreement, caught in the Shade's persuasive spell.

"Oh, I don't think so!" a familiar voice rang out.

Mia blinked. The spell the Shade had been casting faded in an instant. She swung around and saw Violet standing just inside the front gate.

"Violet!" she gasped in astonishment.

Violet put her hands on her hips and gave the Shade a level stare. "Your freedom is over, Shade." She held up her phone. "Smile!"

The Shade's face pulled into a grimace as the camera on her phone flashed. With a scream he dissolved into smoke and was sucked into the screen of the phone.

"Got him!" Violet said triumphantly.

Mia, Sita, and Lexi stared at her open-mouthed.

"Violet?" Mia stammered. "What's going on?"

Violet raised her eyebrows. "Honestly, Mia, I'd have thought even you could figure this out. I'm a Star Friend, too, of course."

A wildcat with cool indigo eyes, a striped tabby coat, and large, pointed ears stalked out of the shadows. "And I'm her Star Animal," she said.

13
Just the Beginning

For once, Mia was at a loss for words. She glanced at Bracken. He looked as shocked as she felt.

Sorrel, the wildcat, looked around. "Well, this is fun," she said, her indigo eyes sparkling with amusement.

"How … how long have you been a Star Friend?" Sita stammered to Violet.

"Since Monday," said Violet. "Just after I saw all of you in the clearing, Sorrel spoke to me."

Bracken turned to Sorrel. "I thought you'd left."

Sorrel gave him a scornful look. "I'm a cat. We don't follow the pack. My instincts told me I should stick around." She purred and rubbed her body against Violet's legs. "And I'm so glad I did."

Violet touched her head. "So am I," she whispered, smiling.

"Violet is exceptionally talented at magic," Sorrel announced smugly. "She's a Spirit Speaker."

"That explains why she managed to get the Shade to look at the camera so easily," said Bracken.

"A piece of quick-thinking," said Sorrel approvingly. "Did I mention she's very clever, too?"

Mia could see why Violet and

Sorrel had bonded! Still, although they were both annoying, Mia couldn't deny that Violet had helped save the day. She shuffled her feet awkwardly. "Well … um … thanks for trapping the Shade," she said.

"Yes, thank you," said Sita. "I don't know what we would have done if you hadn't been here."

Lexi nodded.

Violet shrugged. "It's okay. I'm glad I could help."

Sita kneeled down by Bracken. His side was bleeding. "Here, let me heal you." She touched her hands to the wound, and it closed up.

"Thank you," he said, licking her gratefully.

"What will you do with the Shade now that you've trapped it, Violet?" said Mia.

"You won't be able to use your phone while it's in there," said Bracken.

Violet clicked on the photo, and the girls saw the Shade moving angrily inside the screen.

"Careful!" Juniper burst out.

"I will not be kept in here!" the Shade ranted. "I will not! I—"

"Spirit, return to the shadows," Violet said coolly. "I command it." She pressed DELETE.

For a moment the girls saw the Shade's face screw up in horror, and then the photo vanished.

Violet looked up and gave a grin. "All taken care of," she said.

Sorrel weaved around her legs. "Oh, clever girl. Best of all possible Star Friends."

Lexi made a face at Mia. "Should I be sick now?" she muttered.

"Violet," Sita said. "It's great that you were

able to help … but why were you even here? Did you know about the Shade?"

Violet shook her head. "Not for sure. Sorrel sensed something was wrong—she could smell it in the air—but she wasn't sure exactly what was happening."

Sorrel flicked her tail. "Cats are *far* more sensitive than other Star Animals," she said, giving the other three animals a superior look.

"I actually came over to talk about tomorrow," Violet said. "I've been thinking about the Harvest Show. You're right, Sita— raising as much money as we can is the most important thing, so I wanted to say I'd share a table with you. When I got here, we heard noises and came into the yard."

"Luckily for all of you," said Sorrel tartly. "You weren't handling the Shade very well on your own."

"We were fighting it off," said Bracken defensively.

"Star Friends are meant to trap Shades, not fight them," Sorrel said. "Or had you forgotten that? But I know it's hard without a Spirit Speaker. Luckily you have Violet and me to help you now."

Mia exchanged looks with Lexi and Sita. She was relieved Violet had been there to help them, but she wasn't sure how she felt about Violet and Sorrel hanging out with them regularly and helping them. Meeting her friends' eyes, she could tell they felt the same.

"I'd better get home. We'll see you in the morning," Violet said. "Come on, Sorrel."

"'Bye," said Sita.

"Yeah, 'bye," muttered both Mia and Lexi.

Violet put her hand on Sorrel's head, and the two of them seemed to vanish into thin air.

"Stealth," said Juniper, flicking his tail. "Violet must have that magical ability as well as being able to command spirits."

"Great," said Mia, shaking her head. "So she's doubly talented."

"Which will make her doubly unbearable!" said Lexi. "I don't want to have to work with them."

"It might not be that bad," said Sita hopefully.

"Someone's coming," Willow said, her ears swiveling toward the house.

The animals vanished just as Cleo appeared.

She stood there groggily, swaying slightly. "I feel really strange," she said. "I've just woken up on the couch, but I feel like I've been asleep all day. Did I have an argument with Beth?"

"Yes," Mia said. "You weren't very nice to her."

Cleo bit her lip. "I don't really remember it…." She shook her head. "I feel really dizzy and shaky."

Sita went over and put her hand on Cleo's arm. "You probably have a virus," she said soothingly. "That must have been why you were acting so strangely. I'm sure if you tell Beth that, she'll understand."

Cleo nodded. "I'll call her right away and say how sorry I am."

"Yes, do that," said Sita.

Mia found herself nodding along with Cleo. As Sita was growing stronger, it seemed like she wasn't just able to comfort and heal people, but she was able to persuade them to do things, too.

A puzzled look crossed Cleo's face, and she patted her jeans' pockets. "Has anyone seen my compact?"

Mia bit her lip. "I'm … um … sorry. I

borrowed it and I … well … I broke it." She picked up the compact from the grass and held it out. Cleo looked at the cracked mirror for a moment and then shrugged.

"Okay, well, no big deal. It can go in the garbage."

"She doesn't remember anything about the Shade," hissed Lexi as Cleo went back inside and the animals all reappeared.

Juniper flicked his tail. "No, now that the Shade has been sent back to the Shadows, she won't remember a thing."

Mia yawned and looked up, suddenly realizing that night had fallen and stars were twinkling in the dark sky. "It's been an incredible day," she said.

"A bit too incredible for me," said Sita. "How about we all go and have hot chocolate?"

"Good plan. We can eat some of our midnight snack, too," said Lexi. "I know it's only about seven o'clock, but I think I need to do something normal for a while."

"Normal sounds good," said Sita.

They headed inside. Mia hesitated, looking at the compact in her hand. Now that it was no longer inhabited by a Shade, it was just an ordinary silver and pink compact with a shiny lid and a broken mirror. So much had happened since Aunt Carol had found it at Grandma Anne's. It was so strange to think that Grandma Anne had probably been a Star Friend, too—strange but comforting. *I wonder what's going to happen to us all next,* she thought.

The surface of the case started to shimmer. Mia caught her breath as she saw an image appear in it. It was a picture of herself, Lexi, Sita, and Violet at the bake sale. She was seeing the future! There were a lot of people around their table, the money jar was filling up with coins, and Cleo and Beth were helping them, their argument apparently forgotten. That was good. Then the image changed. Mia saw herself talking to Lexi, Sita, and Violet in the clearing, their faces anxious. The images flashed by—a cave with a circle of candles, a girl holding her ankle and crying, a dark corridor with something moving in the shadows, a burning shed, and then Mia herself with magic surging strongly through her, her hands raised. The images went faster and faster.

Mia. Bracken's voice broke into her thoughts.

She blinked, and the pictures vanished. She took a shaky breath and slipped the compact into her pocket.

Bracken jumped into her arms. "What just happened?" he said softly.

"I think I saw the future," she told him.

"What did you see?" he asked.

"A bunch of things." She hugged him, thinking back over the images. "There's so much we're going to do."

Bracken nuzzled her neck. "I know. *This* is just the beginning, Mia. Someone must have put the Shade in that mirror. We need to find out who it is and stop them before they do anything else. We also have to figure out how to work with Violet and Sorrel."

"I'm so glad I've got you," Mia said, kissing his head.

"You do," he replied, snuggling closer into her arms. "For always. Whatever's waiting."

Mia felt a warm glow tingle through her. As long as she had Bracken, nothing else mattered.

Just then, Lexi popped her head out of the French windows. "Are you two going to stay out there all night?"

"We're coming!" said Mia as the fox jumped down from her arms. With Bracken trotting at her heels, she headed inside to join her friends.